DETROIT
PISTONS

by Joanne C. Gerstner

Printed in the United States of America,
North Mankato, Minnesota
062011
092011

 THIS BOOK CONTAINS AT LEAST 10% RECYCLED MATERIALS.

Editor: Chrös McDougall
Copy Editor: Anna Comstock
Series design and cover production: Christa Schneider
Interior production: Carol Castro

Photo Credits: Duane Burleson/AP Images, cover, 30, 33, 41, 43 (top, bottom); Rick Stewart/Getty Images, 1; Jeff Haynes/AP Images, 4; Mark J. Terrill/AP Images, 7; Michael Conroy/AP Images, 9, 36, 43 (middle); AP Images, 10, 12, 18, 42 (top); GEH/AP Images, 15, 42 (middle); JJL/AP Images, 16; RAS/AP Images, 21; Peter Southwick/AP Images, 22; Mark Duncan/AP Images, 25; Elisa Amendola/AP Images, 27, 42 (bottom); Jennings/AP Images, 28; Aaron Harris/AP Images, 34; Michael Dwyer/AP Images, 39; Lennox McLendon/AP Images, 44; Carlos Osorio/AP Images, 47

Library of Congress Cataloging-in-Publication Data
Gerstner, Joanne, 1971-
  Detroit Pistons / by Joanne C. Gerstner.
      p. cm. -- (Inside the NBA)
  Includes index.
  ISBN 978-1-61783-156-0
  1. Detroit Pistons (Basketball team)--History--Juvenile literature. I. Title.
  GV885.52.D47G47 2012
  796.323'640977434--dc22
                           2011014747

TABLE OF CONTENTS

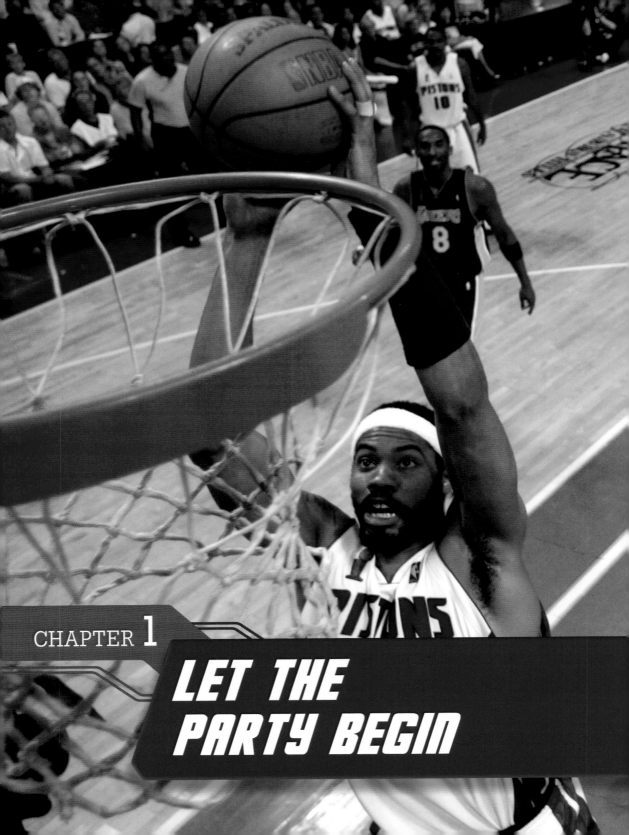

CHAPTER 1

LET THE PARTY BEGIN

S ports fans usually wait until the game is over to start celebrating a title. But the 2004 Detroit Pistons did things their own way, allowing their fans to start the party a bit early at their home arena— the Palace of Auburn Hills.

The Pistons were playing the Los Angeles Lakers in the National Basketball Association (NBA) Finals. The Lakers had been favored to win the championship series, which would have been their fourth in five years. They featured three of the game's best-ever players in guard Kobe Bryant, center Shaquille O'Neal, and power forward Karl Malone.

Instead, a hard-working, team-oriented Pistons team came out stronger. Behind star point guard Chauncey Billups and other key players, such as guard Richard "Rip" Hamilton,

Pistons forward Rasheed Wallace throws down a dunk during the 2004 NBA Finals. He averaged 13 points and 7.8 rebounds in the series.

CHAUNCEY

All Chauncey Billups wanted was to find a team that would let him play. Billups had played for four teams between 1997–98 and 2001–02. He knew he could be a good player, if only he could stay in one place long enough. Pistons president Joe Dumars, himself a former guard for the Pistons, recognized Billups's potential and signed him as a free agent in 2002.

Billups quickly became a fan favorite in Detroit, thanks to his clutch shooting and fun personality. He led the Pistons through the 2003–04 playoffs, averaging 16.4 points and 5.9 assists per game. Billups stayed part of the Pistons starting line-up until 2008, when he was traded to the Denver Nuggets for guard Allen Iverson.

Fans were upset with Dumars for making the trade. Billups said he missed playing for the Pistons, but was happy to be back in his hometown of Denver.

forwards Tayshaun Prince and Rasheed Wallace, and center Ben Wallace, the Pistons had taken a 3–1 series lead going into Game 5 at home.

The Pistons and the Lakers dueled evenly during the first two quarters of Game 5. Then the Pistons shifted into another gear. Bryant and O'Neal were powerless against the swarming Pistons defense and its dominant rebounding. Malone had an injured knee and did not play. When the Pistons built an 82–59 lead by the end of the third quarter, fans began celebrating.

"Beat L.A.!" and "Bad Boys!" chants rang out from the approximately 21,000 fans in attendance. They could sense that the Pistons were about to win their first NBA championship since 1990.

The crowd noise grew louder by the minute until the

The Pistons' Rip Hamilton drives against the Los Angeles Lakers during the 2004 NBA Finals. Hamilton led the Pistons with 21.4 points per game.

final horn sounded. The Pistons won, 100–87, and captured their third NBA title. They became the first Eastern Conference team to win an NBA title since the Chicago Bulls had done it in 1998. The Lakers and the San Antonio Spurs of the Western Conference had dominated the NBA ever since.

"We did it," said Billups, who was named the Finals Most Valuable Player (MVP). "We came into this series, nobody gave us a chance, but we felt we had a great chance. . . . We just felt we were a better team."

The Pistons' players ran onto the floor, hugging each other and yelling. Pistons coach

'Sheed

Nobody knew what Pistons power forward Rasheed Wallace was going to do or say next. At times, he even surprised himself. Wallace was traded to the Pistons in February 2004 and quickly became a key player—and personality. He could make a big play, such as hitting a three-pointer or blocking a shot. He also was bold enough to make predictions. He "guaran-Sheed"— Wallace's term for a personal promise—that the Pistons would beat the Indiana Pacers in Game 2 of the 2004 Eastern Conference finals. The Pistons did indeed win the game—and the series.

Larry Brown hugged his assistant coaches—among them was his older brother Herb Brown—and celebrated the first NBA title of his long coaching career.

Brown had become a celebrated basketball coach during his long career on the bench. But he was also known as a coach who switched teams frequently. He had coached three college teams and seven professional teams before he came to the Pistons in 2003–04.

The Pistons had a good team with many veteran players when Brown took over. Those players had guided Detroit to the conference finals the year before. But under Brown, everything came together. Although no Pistons players were superstars on the level of Bryant or O'Neal, they emerged as a new power in the NBA by stressing teamwork and defense.

The championship party spilled out into the arena's parking lot and onto the streets of Detroit and its suburbs. People drove around in their cars, honking their horns and yelling into the warm summer night.

The Pistons' party would go on into the early morning hours. Billups, along with his good friend Hamilton, were among the last ones left in the arena. As the lights were being

Pistons center Ben Wallace, *left*, holds the NBA Championship Trophy while point guard Chauncey Billups, *right*, holds the Finals MVP Trophy after the Pistons beat the Lakers in the 2004 NBA Finals.

turned off for the night, the pair was spied on a ladder, taking turns cutting down one of the basketball nets and laughing. The dream had come true: they were NBA champions.

One of a Kind

When the Pistons won the 2003–04 NBA title, Larry Brown became the first coach to have won an NBA championship and a collegiate national championship. He had previously guided the University of Kansas to a national title in 1988.

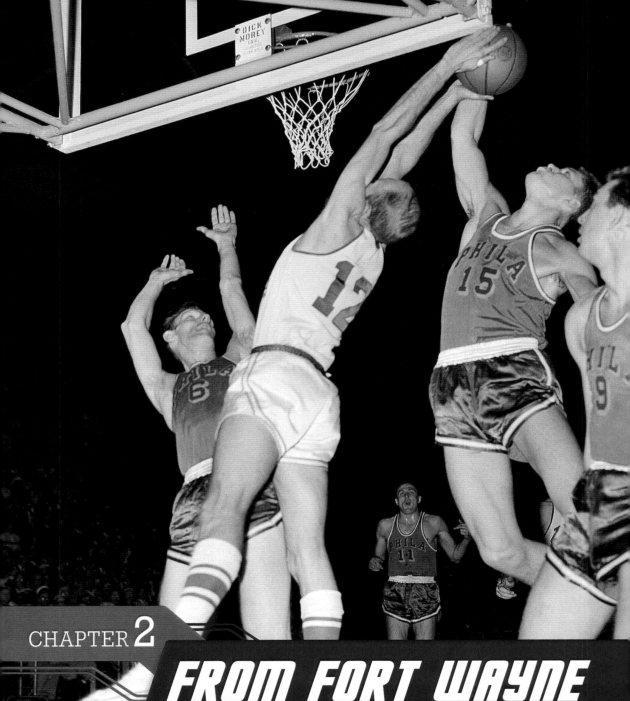

CHAPTER **2**

FROM FORT WAYNE TO DETROIT

Businessman Fred Zollner was a very busy person. He owned a successful company, based in Fort Wayne, Indiana, that made parts for cars, buses, and small engines during the 1930s. The parts were called pistons.

Zollner also loved basketball. He noticed that he had a lot of good basketball players working in his factory. One day, Zollner had an idea: Why not create his own basketball team? In 1937, he started an amateur team to play games against other company-sponsored teams. Zollner's team was named after the important part made by his company: the Pistons.

"We rarely lost," Zollner said. "And since we were playing neighboring industries, we were making enemies instead of friends."

The team proved to be popular among fans, which led Zollner to another idea: Why not make the Pistons a professional

Fort Wayne Pistons forward George Yardley, *in white*, grabs an offensive rebound against the Philadelphia Warriors during the 1956 playoffs.

George Yardley drives between St. Louis Hawks players during a 1957 game. He played five-plus seasons with the Pistons.

basketball team? So the Fort Wayne Zollner Pistons were created in 1941. They joined a league called the National Basketball League (NBL).

What Is a Piston?

A piston is an important part of an engine that helps machines run. Pistons are metal cylinders that pump up and down, helping mix and move air and gas through machines.

Zollner took his team's success very seriously. He watched college games to find the top young players. Then he gave them contracts, allowing the players to work for his Zollner Machine Works Company during the day, and play basketball for the Zollner Pistons at night.

The Zollner Pistons became one of the NBL's best teams. Guard Bobby McDermott was the team's first star player. Basketball was often played at a very slow pace during that era. But McDermott was able to dominate with his speed and great scoring abilities. He joined the Zollner Pistons in 1941 and led them to the 1944 and 1945 NBL championships.

Despite his team's success in the NBL, Zollner recognized that there were too many small basketball leagues around the country. Being a businessman, he figured that it would be best for all of the small leagues to combine into one big league.

Zollner soon helped convince the NBL and the Basketball Association of America to see things his way. The leagues merged in 1949, creating the modern NBA.

The new NBA was a tough league. There were now many strong teams in competition

FRED ZOLLNER

Fred Zollner always wanted the Pistons to be the best and most popular team in the league, so he did a number of creative things that were unheard of at the time to achieve that fame. For instance, in the early days NBA players rode in trains and buses to get to their games. Sometimes the journey would take many hours because of distance and weather. Zollner realized his players would be better rested and have a stronger chance of winning if he could make travel easier. So, in 1952 he started flying the Pistons to their away games. They were the first NBA team to do that. Today, every team flies to away games. Zollner also held a number of promotions to try to attract fans. For one, kids were admitted for pennies to Pistons games in Detroit.

Zollner sold the Pistons in 1974. He was inducted into the Naismith Basketball Hall of Fame in 1999. Zollner died in 1982, at age 81.

George Yardley

George Yardley became the Pistons' first superstar when he joined the NBA. Yardley had a flashy, dramatic style that thrilled fans. He was also an effective scorer. In 1957–58 he became the first player in NBA history to score 2,000 points in one season. Yardley played for the Pistons for six seasons and was a six-time All-Star. He retired in 1960, at the age of 31, and was inducted in the Naismith Basketball Hall of Fame in 1996. He died in 2004, at age 75.

with each other. The newly-named Fort Wayne Pistons were put into the NBA's strong Central Division. Among the other good teams in the Central were the Minneapolis Lakers from Minnesota and the Rochester Royals from New York.

The Pistons were no longer one of the best teams. Although they always made the playoffs, they did not finish higher than third place in their division during the first five years of the NBA. The Lakers and the Royals traded first and second places each year. That did not deter the Pistons, though.

Thanks to Zollner's sharp eye for talent, the Pistons continued to add good players during those seasons. Among them was forward George Yardley, whom the team drafted in 1950. Yardley played a key role in helping the Pistons return to the top.

The Pistons finally broke through in 1954–55. Led by Yardley's scoring, the Pistons won their division and advanced all the way to the NBA Finals. However, they lost to the Syracuse Nationals in a seven-game series. The Pistons returned to the Finals in 1955–56. This time they lost to the Philadelphia Warriors in five games.

Even though the championship eluded them, the Pistons had returned to their

The Pistons' Dick McGuire charges down the court during a 1958 game against the Minneapolis Lakers.

position as one of the top teams. However, along the way Zollner had noticed something. The teams in larger cities, such as Philadelphia and Minneapolis, were drawing much larger crowds than the Pistons were in Fort Wayne. In order for his team to keep up, Zollner realized that he would have to move it to a larger city.

Zollner had visited Detroit, Michigan, many times, as many of the parts his company made were sold to the big automobile companies there. Zollner liked what he saw in the city and moved his team to Michigan in 1957–58. The Fort Wayne Pistons turned into the Detroit Pistons, and a new era of basketball in a new city began.

CHAPTER 3

SOME STARS, BUT MOSTLY STRUGGLES

The Pistons found a new home in Detroit. However, it would take nearly three decades before the team would be counted as an NBA title contender. The Pistons posted a losing record every season from 1957–58 through 1969–70.

There was some benefit to the losing, though. All of the losing seasons helped the Pistons stockpile some of the league's best young players through the draft. That is because the top draft picks are awarded to the league's worst teams.

Future Hall of Famers guard Dave Bing, center Bob Lanier, and guard/forward Dave DeBusschere were all drafted by the Pistons between 1960 and 1970. And all three became fan favorites because they worked hard, displayed good sportsmanship, played good defense, and scored a lot of points. DeBusschere was especially loved, because he had grown up in Detroit.

Pistons guard Dave Bing looks for a teammate to pass to during a 1967 game against the Los Angeles Lakers.

Dave DeBusschere attempts a rebound during a 1968 game. The Detroit native played his first 6 1/2 seasons with the Pistons.

Bing

Dave Bing was an unlikely basketball player. He overcame a serious childhood eye injury to become a smooth-shooting guard. Bing was the 1966–67 Rookie of the Year after averaging 20 points per game. He was a six-time All-Star over his nine years with the Pistons, and was later elected to the Naismith Basketball Hall of Fame. Bing stayed in Detroit after he retired and established a successful steel company. He was elected mayor of Detroit in 2009.

Having a few special players was not enough to make the Pistons a good team. There were low points. One of them was the 1963–64 season, when the Pistons finished 23–57. Things were just as bad in 1965–66, when the Pistons lost 58 games. That was the most losses in the team's history since it had been in Detroit.

Upon arriving in Detroit, the Pistons shared Olympia Arena with the Red Wings of the National Hockey league. After four years, they moved to Cobo Arena in downtown Detroit.

Despite their poor records, the Pistons did make the play-offs a few times during the 1960s and 1970s. But they never advanced past the second round. The Pistons' best season during that era was 1973–74, when they finished 52–30. However, they lost to the Chicago Bulls in the first round of the playoffs.

Fred Zollner grew tired of the losing and the pressure of running the Pistons. He sold the team in 1974 to a group led by Detroit businessman Bill Davidson. Zollner and Davidson shared a love of basketball, and both had become wealthy making car parts.

LOCAL HERO

Dave DeBusschere grew up on Detroit's East Side as a star football, baseball, and basketball player. In college, he starred for the University of Detroit baseball and basketball teams. In 1962, the Pistons selected him in the NBA Draft, and the Chicago White Sox signed him to play baseball. DeBusschere decided to pursue both sports. He played for the Pistons and also for the White Sox and their minor league clubs. In 1965, he turned his focus to basketball.

Pistons owner Fred Zollner liked DeBusschere's tough attitude on the court. So Zollner made a desperate move in 1964. He named the 24-year-old DeBusschere as the Pistons' player and coach. The big change did not help the Pistons start winning. DeBusschere resigned as coach after three years with a 79–143 record. He was traded to the New York Knicks in 1968 and was voted into the Hall of Fame in 1983.

The Big Man

Center Bob Lanier showed a lot of promise with his imposing 6-foot-11 frame, so the Pistons selected him first overall in the 1970 draft. Lanier proved to be a dominant player, using his size and athletic talent to rule the paint. He played for nine years with the Pistons, and through 2010–11 still holds many of the team's records for scoring average, rebounding, and points. Lanier averaged 22.7 points per game, pulled down 8,063 rebounds, and scored a total of 15,488 points in his time with the Pistons. He was inducted into the Basketball Hall of Fame in 1992.

Davidson knew he had to shake things up in order to rebuild the Pistons into a winning team. He hired and fired coaches frequently, trying to find the right leader. The Pistons were also busy trading players, trying to get a young, aggressive team. They traded Bing in 1975, then Lanier in 1980. Zollner had traded away DeBusschere in 1968.

By the 1980s, Davidson was starting to find the right mix. A new coach named Chuck Daly was hired in 1983. During that time, the Pistons also drafted important players for the future, including guards Isiah Thomas (1981) and Joe Dumars (1985), as well as forwards Kelly Tripucka (1981), John Salley (1986), and Dennis Rodman (1986).

The team had moved from Cobo Arena to the Pontiac Silverdome in Detroit's suburbs in 1979. By the late 1980s, Davidson was hoping to build the team a new arena meant just for basketball. He would soon get that stadium, and one of the NBA's best teams to go with it.

Pistons center Bob Lanier attempts a hook shot against the Houston Rockets during a 1978 game at Cobo Arena.

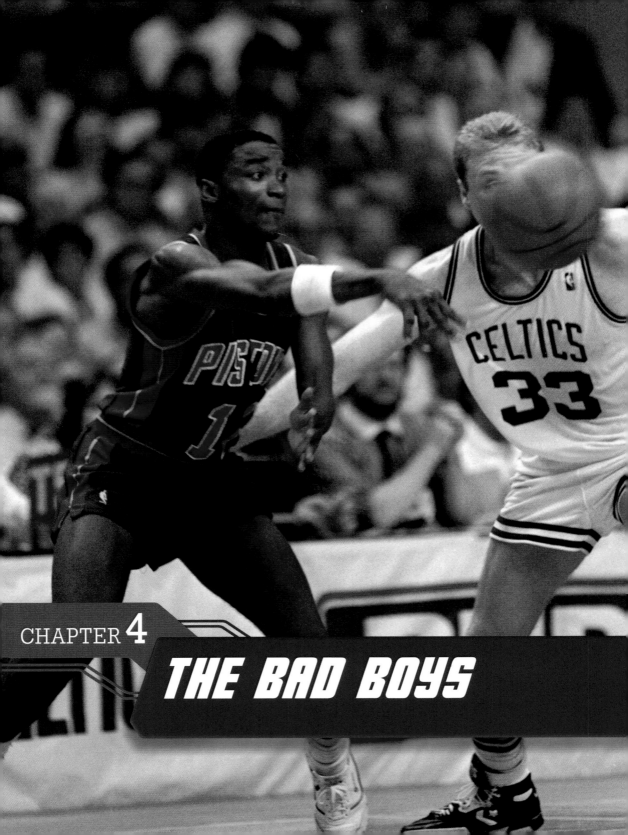

CHAPTER 4

THE BAD BOYS

The Pistons were starting to become known for their tough, physical, and defensive-minded play by the mid-1980s. And they were also starting to win. Some people did not like the Pistons, though. They thought the team's intimidating style was too rough and mean. For that physical playing style, the Pistons were nicknamed the "Bad Boys."

Coach Chuck Daly did not mind the critics. He liked having strong players on the court. Star point guard Isiah Thomas was the leader. Daly also liked a little bit of intimidation. He wanted opposing teams to be a little afraid of his Pistons. With bruising big men Bill Laimbeer and Rick Mahorn roughing up opposing players, Daly got his wish there, too.

With the pieces in place to execute Daly's playing style, the Pistons began to make a move. They reached the Eastern

Point guard Isiah Thomas became the Pistons' leader during the 1980s and early 1990s. He was known for his grit and toughness, despite being only 6-foot-1.

STAR BACKCOURT

Isiah Thomas and Joe Dumars combined to make one of the NBA's best backcourts during their nine seasons together in Detroit. Thomas quickly won over Pistons fans when he arrived in 1981. He had a winning smile and loved to laugh. But make no mistake—Thomas was one of the toughest players on the court. He played for the Pistons for 13 years, becoming the team's all-time leader in points (18,822), field goals made (7,194), free throws made (4,036), assists (9,061), and steals (1,861).

The Pistons drafted Dumars in 1985–86. He was also known for his tough defense, as well as his ability to shoot from long range. Through 2010–11, he still held team records for three-pointers made (600) and attempted (2,592), as well as games played for the team (1,018). Dumars played through 1999 before moving to the Pistons' front office.

Both Thomas and Dumars were inducted into the Hall of Fame.

Conference finals in 1986–87, but lost to the Boston Celtics in seven close games. It was a tough lesson, but Daly saw hope for the future.

"We are going to accomplish something this franchise has never had: an NBA championship," Daly told reporters.

The Pistons got one step closer to that in 1987–88. They advanced all the way to the NBA Finals that year. However, they lost a tight seven-game series to the Los Angeles Lakers.

Detroit was ready to take that final step in 1988–89. The Pistons began the season in a new home, having moved into the Palace of Auburn Hills. They immediately had success in the new arena. The Pistons won 63 games that season—a team record.

The Bad Boys then set out to claim the title they had

Center Bill Laimbeer, *right*, and the Pistons of the late 1980s and early 1990s were known as the "Bad Boys" for their physical play.

fallen just short of in the previous season. Detroit did not lose a game during the first two rounds of the playoffs. It took six games for the Pistons to win the conference championship, beating an emerging Chicago Bulls team that featured a young Michael Jordan and Scottie Pippen. This was the Pistons' time, though. They

Baddest Boys

Big men Bill Laimbeer and Rick Mahorn might not have been the biggest stars on the Pistons' Bad Boys teams, but they might have been the toughest. Laimbeer had a good jumper, and Mahorn could be counted on for rebounds. But they were most well known for their intimidating play. Mahorn left the Pistons in the expansion draft before the 1989–90 season; Laimbeer retired in 1993.

were headed to the NBA Finals for a rematch with the Lakers.

The rematch was never close. The Pistons swept the Lakers in four games, thanks to the hot shooting of guard Joe Dumars. He averaged 27.3 points per game during the series and was named the Finals MVP.

The Pistons lost starting forward Rick Mahorn in the expansion draft during the off-season. The Bad Boys were not finished, though. They came back and won 59 games in 1989–90. Then they rolled through the playoffs without losing a home game. This time, they faced the Portland Trail Blazers in the NBA Finals.

The teams split the first two games, but Thomas and the Pistons took over after that. Detroit won the next three games and their second straight NBA championship. Thomas averaged 27.6 points per game on his way to the Finals MVP trophy.

A reporter asked Thomas if winning a second title was as fun as the first one.

"Was this sweeter than last time? It was, because people doubted we could do it this time," Thomas said. "We're not as physically talented as we were last year. But we're smarter."

Life was good for Pistons fans. After a slow start in the

The Palace of Auburn Hills

Pistons owner Bill Davidson used his own money to build an arena to house his basketball team and host events. The Palace opened in 1988, just in time to host the Bad Boys' three consecutive trips to the NBA Finals. It has also hosted four Women's National Basketball Association Finals, with the Detroit Shock winning three titles. The arena holds 22,076 fans for basketball games. It also hosts many concerts.

Forward Dennis Rodman lifts Isiah Thomas into the air after the Pistons won Game 1 of the 1990 NBA Finals. Detroit won the series in five games.

NBA, the Pistons had emerged as the league's most feared team—in more ways than one. But the Pistons' days on top were numbered, and it would take more than a decade before the team would again be a championship contender.

CHAPTER **5**

THE LETDOWN

Pistons fans developed high expectations after the Bad Boys won back-to-back titles. They figured the team would stick together and keep winning. But things did not work that way. Part of that was because of changes within the Pistons organization. Part of it also had to do with the emergence of the Chicago Bulls.

Coach Chuck Daly left the Pistons after the 1991–92 season. Soon after, injuries, trades, and retirements began to split up the once-proud Bad Boys. Isiah Thomas and Bill Laimbeer both retired in 1994. By the start of the 1994–95 season, other Bad Boys such as Dennis Rodman, John Salley, and Rick Mahorn were gone as well. Only Joe Dumars remained with the Pistons as the team changed its roster to become younger and faster.

Meanwhile, the Bulls began to take control of not just the Eastern Conference but

Pistons forward Dennis Rodman pulls down a rebound during a 1993 game. Rodman led the NBA with 18.3 rebounds per game that season.

Grant Hill starred for the Pistons from 1994 to 2000, but he was never able to lead the team back to an NBA title.

also the entire NBA. Behind superstars Michael Jordan and Scottie Pippen, the Bulls won the NBA championship in each of the three years after Detroit's 1990 triumph.

As the Bulls propelled to the top, the Pistons fell toward the bottom. The low point was in 1993–94, when they finished 20–62. That was tied for the worst record in the Eastern Conference and tied for second-worst in the NBA. It was the Pistons' worst record since 1980.

The Pistons did have some consolation, though. Because of their bad record, they picked third overall in that year's draft. With that pick they selected guard/forward Grant Hill out of Duke University.

Hill became a bright spot for the Pistons, even though the team only finished 28–54 during the 1994–95 season. He was a natural scorer who was able to drive and shoot easily. Hill was named the NBA co-Rookie of the Year thanks to his average of 19.9 points per game.

Behind Hill, the Pistons slowly improved over the next few years, reaching the playoffs each season. They had a winning record again in 1995–96. They improved to 54–28 the next year. That was their best record since winning 59 games in 1989–90. However, the Pistons were eliminated in the first round of the playoffs each time.

After missing the postseason in 1997–98, the Pistons were back the next season. Hill continued to improve and had his best season with the Pistons in 1999–2000. He averaged 25.8 points per game. Dumars had retired during the off-season. But behind Hill and other stars such as guard Lindsey Hunter and swingman Jerry Stackhouse, the Pistons finished 42–40 that season.

However, things changed for Hill and the Pistons on April 15, 2000. Hill was playing against the Philadelphia

Grant Hill

Fans quickly took to Grant Hill, who had a warm personality and did a lot of work for charity. But the end of his time in Detroit was a difficult one for the team and its fans. Some fans were angry with Hill for wanting to leave the Pistons. Others, however, were happy to see him leave. They thought his best days were behind him because of his ankle problems. It turned out to be a little of both. Hill's ankle injuries caused him problems until 2004. Eventually, though, Hill returned to full strength and became a key player for the Orlando Magic, and later, the Phoenix Suns.

CHUCK DALY

Chuck Daly once was a high school teacher in Punxsutawney, Pennsylvania—the town that hosts the annual Groundhog Day ceremony. He seemed like an unlikely person to be an NBA coach, but he knew how to manage players and get the best out of them.

Daly helped develop the tough, defensive style that became the strength of the Bad Boys teams that won two NBA championships. And he was so well respected as the Pistons' coach that he was picked to be Team USA's basketball coach for the 1992 Olympic Games in Barcelona, Spain.

Daly left the Pistons after the 1991–92 season. He coached four more seasons with the New Jersey Nets and the Orlando Magic. He remained close to the Pistons, though, often attending playoff games or coming back for special events. He was inducted into the Naismith Basketball Hall of Fame in 1994. He died in 2009 at age 78.

76ers in one of the last regular season games when he hurt his left ankle. Pistons doctors said he had a sprain. But the ankle did not heal as expected. It continued to hurt Hill into the playoffs. He only played the first two of three games as the Pistons were again eliminated in the first round of the playoffs. It turned out Hill had a more serious injury. He needed surgery to repair broken bones in his foot.

At that point, Hill decided he wanted to leave the Pistons and go to the Orlando Magic. The Pistons worked out a deal in which Hill would sign a new contract with them, and then immediately be traded to the Magic. In return, the Pistons got guard Chucky Atkins and center Ben Wallace.

The once-promising Grant Hill era did not lead the Pistons past the first round

Joe Dumars was the last of the Bad Boys. He played for the Pistons from 1985 to 1999 before taking a job in the team's front office.

of the playoffs before they were rebuilding once again. Dumars, who was now working in the Pistons' front office, was in charge of finding a new winning combination. Success would come sooner than even Dumars thought.

Did You Know?

The NBA awards a trophy every year to a player who displays sportsmanship and respect. The NBA Sportsmanship Award was renamed in 2000 after Joe Dumars, honoring his years of playing with sportsmanship. Dumars was the first player to win the award, in 1996.

CHAPTER 6

GOING UP, THEN DOWN AGAIN

Joe Dumars was a star basketball player, helping the Pistons win back-to-back NBA championships. After his playing days ended, he proved to be a smart basketball executive as well. Dumars had a vision for the Pistons. He wanted the team to focus on the things that made his Bad Boys teams successful: tough defense, hard work, and mental toughness.

In the Pistons' front office, Dumars started making careful trades and draft choices. One by one, the pieces came together for a championship basketball team. The Pistons added center Ben Wallace, one of the league's most feared defenders, in the Grant Hill trade in 2000. In 2002, they drafted forward Tayshaun Prince, signed free agent point guard Chauncey Billups, and traded for shooting guard Richard "Rip" Hamilton.

The Pistons were quickly rising to the top of the Eastern

The Pistons added center Ben Wallace in 2000. He became one of the key pieces in the team's title run in 2003–04.

Pistons players congratulate coach Larry Brown after the team beat the Los Angeles Lakers in Game 5 of the 2004 NBA Finals.

Conference. After falling to 32–50 in 2000–01, Detroit went 50–32 in 2001–02. It was the first of seven straight seasons of winning at least 50 games. As they improved, the Pistons began to resemble the hard-working, defensive-minded team that Dumars envisioned.

Detroit repeated with a 50–32 record in 2002–03. And, for the first time since 1990–91,

they also reached the Eastern Conference finals. But it was not to be this time. The New Jersey Nets swept the Pistons in four games. It was a learning experience, though. And just like the Bad Boys had done in the late 1980s, the team built upon its near miss.

The Pistons largely brought the same team back for 2003–04. There was one big change, though: coach Larry Brown. Under Brown, everything seemed to come together for the Pistons. They won 54 games and intimidated teams with their workmanlike play. Billups, Hamilton, and Wallace were stars, with Prince and forward Mehmet Okur adding support.

The mid-season addition of forward Rasheed Wallace was the final piece the Pistons needed. He was known for being a talented but emotional player. He had struggled to control his emotions in the past, but his energy immediately brought a spark to the Pistons.

"He made our team better in every way," Brown said. "I think most people felt when he got here that he would be a defensive force, and he was in many ways. But his presence defensively, with Ben [Wallace] and Tayshaun [Prince] gave

Ben Wallace

When Virginia Union center Ben Wallace entered the 1996 NBA Draft, no team selected him. They thought that at 6-foot-9, he was too short to play center in the NBA. But Wallace proved everybody wrong. Through 2010–11, the athletic center was the NBA's Defensive Player of the Year four times, and has been an All-Star four times. He played for the Pistons from 2000–01 through 2005–06 and rejoined the team in 2009–10. When Wallace, who is nicknamed "Big Ben," makes a big play at the Palace of Auburn Hills, a bell tolls, just like in the famous Big Ben clock tower in London, England.

us unbelievable shot-blocking, quickness, and unselfish play."

With their team set, the Pistons went on to reach the NBA Finals for the first time in 14 years. Their teamwork and hustling play helped them shock the reigning champion Los Angeles Lakers four games to one for their third NBA title.

"Every guy contributed, from the first man to the twelfth

THE MALICE AT THE PALACE

The events of November 14, 2004, at the Palace of Auburn Hills dramatically changed the future of the Pistons, the Indiana Pacers, and the NBA. With the Pacers comfortably leading late in a regular season game, Indiana forward Ron Artest fouled Ben Wallace hard as he went for a basket. Tensions boiled over as Wallace shoved Artest, resulting in a fight between the teams.

Artest tried to escape the fight by lying on the scorer's table. However, when a fan threw a cup that landed on Artest's chest, chaos erupted. Artest raced into the stands and began punching the fan whom he thought had thrown it. Another Pacers player followed him into the stands. Later, Artest and other Pacers players punched Pistons fans who had come onto the court.

The game was called. Nine players between the teams were suspended for a combined 140 games.

man," Rasheed Wallace said. "That's what gave us so much energy. That's what sparked our effort."

The Pistons remained a top team following their third NBA championship. They entered the 2004–05 season with their roster largely intact and hopes of back-to-back titles. They again won 54 games and again reached the NBA Finals. This time, however, they lost to the San Antonio Spurs in a tight seven-game series. Game 7 was played in San Antonio. After the Spurs won 81–74, many of the Pistons were so upset they had tears in their eyes.

The Pistons entered the 2005–06 season with their core players intact, but with one major change. Brown had been fired as coach and replaced by Flip Saunders. It looked like a strong fit, as the Pistons won

Guard Rip Hamilton reacts to a call during the 2008 Eastern Conference finals. The Pistons lost to the Boston Celtics four games to two.

a team-record 64 games during the regular season. They went into the playoffs as the top seed in the Eastern Conference. However, the Pistons fell short when Dwyane Wade, Shaquille O'Neal, and the Miami Heat beat them four games to two in the conference finals.

The Pistons began to fall apart soon after that. Stalwart center Ben Wallace left for the Chicago Bulls in 2006. Billups, the reliable point guard, was traded to the Denver Nuggets in 2008. And sparkplug Rasheed Wallace went to the Boston Celtics in 2009.

Detroit still returned to the Eastern Conference finals in 2006–07 and 2007–08. That marked six consecutive years of reaching the NBA's final four.

Oops

The Pistons had the number two draft pick going into the 2003 NBA Draft, which they had received as part of a 1996 trade. When the Cleveland Cavaliers selected LeBron James with the first pick, Detroit picked Darko Milicic, a relatively unknown 7-foot, 18-year-old center with a good outside shot. He played a very limited role off the bench for the Pistons over the next two and a half seasons and was then traded. Meanwhile, several players selected after Milicic in the 2003 draft went on to All-Star careers, including Carmelo Anthony, Dwyane Wade, and Chris Bosh.

However, by the end, the Pistons were a shell of the team that had won the 2003–04 NBA title.

Saunders was fired after the 2007–08 season and replaced by Michael Curry. The Pistons quickly dropped after that. They made the playoffs in 2008–09, but with a losing record of 39–43. That was 20 fewer wins than the year before. Curry was let go after just one season and replaced by John Kuester. Center Ben Wallace also returned to Detroit, hoping to finish his career with the Pistons. The team's decline only continued, though, as Detroit fell to 27–55 and missed the playoffs for the first time in eight seasons. The Pistons missed the playoffs again in 2010–11 with a 30–52 record.

Just seven years removed from the Pistons' third NBA title, Dumars found himself in a familiar position: trying to rebuild the Pistons.

Forward Tayshaun Prince blocks a shot against the Sacramento Kings in 2011. He has been a top defensive player for Detroit since 2002.

TIMELINE

1937	Businessman Fred Zollner starts an amateur basketball team called the Fort Wayne Zollner Pistons.
1941	The Zollner Pistons turn professional, joining the NBL.
1948	The Pistons join the Basketball Association of America, which turns into the NBA in 1949.
1955	The Pistons lose to the Syracuse Nationals in the NBA Finals, four games to three.
1956	The Pistons lose to the Philadelphia Warriors in the NBA Finals, four games to one.
1957	The Pistons move from Fort Wayne to Detroit.
1974	Zollner sells the team to a group led by Detroit businessman Bill Davidson on July 29.
1981	The Pistons draft Isiah Thomas with the second overall pick in the NBA Draft.
1988	The Pistons lose to the Los Angeles Lakers, four games to three, in the NBA Finals.
1989	The Pistons sweep the Lakers to win their first NBA title since moving to Detroit. Joe Dumars is the MVP.
1990	The Pistons defeat the Portland Trail Blazers, four games to one, to repeat as NBA champions. Thomas is the MVP.

1994	Thomas retires following the 1993–94 season. The Pistons select Grant Hill with the third overall pick in the 1994 NBA Draft.
1999	Dumars retires as a player and moves into the Pistons' front office as an executive.
2000	The Pistons trade Grant Hill to the Orlando Magic on August 3 for Ben Wallace and Chucky Atkins.
2003	The Pistons reach their first Eastern Conference finals since 1991, and start a streak of six consecutive appearances at that level.
2003	The Pistons name Larry Brown as coach on June 2, after Rick Carlisle is fired.
2004	The Pistons win the NBA championship, defeating the Lakers four games to one. Billups is the Finals MVP.
2005	The Pistons lose in the NBA Finals, four games to three, to the San Antonio Spurs.
2005	Brown is fired by the Pistons on July 19 and Flip Saunders is named as the new coach.
2008	After leading the Pistons to the Eastern Conference finals—the sixth consecutive season the team got at least that far—Saunders is fired and replaced by Michael Curry.
2011	Under second-year coach John Kuester, the Pistons finish 30–52 and miss the playoffs for the second year in a row.

QUICK STATS

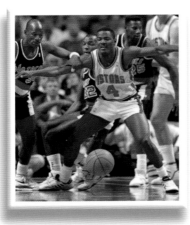

FRANCHISE HISTORY
Fort Wayne Pistons (1948–57)
Detroit Pistons (1957–)

NBA FINALS
(1948–; wins in bold)

1955, 1956, 1988, **1989, 1990, 2004**, 2005

CONFERENCE FINALS
(1971–)

1987, 1988, 1989, 1990, 1991, 2003, 2004, 2005, 2006, 2007, 2008

DIVISION TITLES
(1971–)

1988, 1989, 1990, 2002, 2003, 2005, 2006, 2007, 2008

KEY PLAYERS
(position[s]; years with team)

Chauncey Billups (G; 2002–08)
Dave Bing (G; 1966–75)
Dave DeBusschere (F/G; 1962–68)
Joe Dumars (G; 1985–99)
Richard "Rip" Hamilton (G; 2002–)
Grant Hill (G/F; 1994–2000)
Bill Laimbeer (C; 1981–93)
Bob Lanier (C; 1970–80)
Dennis Rodman (F; 1986–93)
Isiah Thomas (G; 1981–94)
Ben Wallace (C; 2001–06, 2009–)
George Yardley (F; 1953–59)

KEY COACHES
Chuck Daly (1983–92):
    467–271; 71–42 (postseason)
Larry Brown (2003–05):
    108–56; 31–17 (postseason)

HOME ARENAS
North Side High School Gym
    (1947–52)
Allen County War Memorial
    Coliseum (1953–57)
Olympia Arena (1957–61)
Cobo Arena (1961–78)
Pontiac Silverdome (1979–88)
The Palace of Auburn Hills (1988–)

*All statistics through 2010–11 season

QUOTES AND ANECDOTES

The Pistons have had players with some interesting nicknames throughout the years. Chauncey Billups was known as "Smooth," because of his playing style. Ben Wallace was known as "Big Ben," a spin on his first name and a reference to the famous tall clock tower in London. Vinnie Johnson was "The Microwave" because he "heated up" quickly by scoring points. Richard Hamilton commonly went by "Rip." His dad called him that because he ripped off his diapers as a baby. Dennis Rodman was "The Worm" because of how flexible he was while playing. Ron Lee was called "Tasmanian Devil" because he was constantly in motion. And Chuck Daly was "Daddy Rich" because of his classy style of dress in suits.

Center Bob Lanier holds the record for the Pistons player with the biggest shoe size—22.

Larry Brown, who was the Pistons' coach when they won the 2003–04 NBA championship, did not know how moving it would be to win his first title. "Chuck Daly told me one time when you win a title, you won't appreciate it until you're driving down the highway one day and you will get a big grin on your face," Brown said. "I am sure that's how it's going to be for me."

"You know, me and the City of Detroit, we kind of formed a bond with each other. This was meant to be." —Pistons Center Ben Wallace, on what winning the 2003–04 NBA title meant to him

GLOSSARY

amateur

Unpaid.

assist

A pass that leads directly to a made basket.

attendance

The number of fans at a particular game or who come to watch a team play during a particular season.

backcourt

The point guards and shooting guards on a basketball team.

contract

A binding agreement about, for example, years of commitment by a basketball player in exchange for a given salary.

draft

A system used by professional sports leagues to select new players in order to spread incoming talent among all teams. The NBA Draft is held each June.

expansion

In sports, the addition of a franchise or franchises to a league.

franchise

An entire sports organization, including the players, coaches, and staff.

free agent

A player whose contract has expired and who is able to sign with a team of his choice.

general manager

The executive who is in charge of the team's overall operation. He or she hires and fires coaches, drafts players, and signs free agents.

postseason

The games in which the best teams play after the regular-season schedule has been completed.

rebound

To secure the basketball after a missed shot.

FOR MORE INFORMATION

Further Reading

Ballard, Chris. *The Art of a Beautiful Game: The Thinking Fan's Tour of the NBA*. New York: Simon & Schuster, 2009.

Farrell, Perry A. *Tales from the Detroit Pistons*. Champaign, IL: Sports Publishing LLC, 2004.

Simmons, Bill. *The Book of Basketball: The NBA According to the Sports Guy*. New York: Random House, 2009.

Web Links

To learn more about the Detroit Pistons, visit ABDO Publishing Company online at **www.abdopublishing.com**. Web sites about the Pistons are featured on our Book Links page. These links are routinely monitored and updated to provide the most current information available.

Places to Visit

Michigan Sports Hall of Fame
1 Washington Boulevard
Detroit, MI 48226-4420
248-473-0656
www.michigansportshof.org
This hall of fame honors the most influential sportspeople in Michigan history. Many former Pistons are enshrined.

Naismith Memorial Basketball Hall of Fame
1000 West Columbus Avenue
Springfield, MA 01105
413-781-6500
www.hoophall.com
This hall of fame and museum highlights the greatest players and moments in the history of basketball. Joe Dumars and Dave Bing are among the former Pistons enshrined here.

The Palace of Auburn Hills
6 Championship Drive
Auburn Hills, MI 48326
248-377-0100
www.palacenet.com
This has been the Pistons' home arena since 1988. The arena is only open to visitors during events and Pistons games.

INDEX

About the Author

Joanne C. Gerstner is an award-winning sports journalist. Her work has appeared in the *New York Times*, *USA Today*, the *Miami Herald*, and the *Detroit News*. She also appears on ESPN as an expert guest. Gerstner has covered the biggest sporting events in the world, reporting from the Olympic Games, World Cup, tennis and golf US Opens, the NBA Finals, the Stanley Cup Finals, and the Super Bowl. She has lived in Detroit for most of her life.